Grief
Abdul Waheed

Grief

Abdul Waheed

Awarded to
Abdul Waheed
for publishing "Grief"

PUBLISHED
AUTHOR
notionpress.com
CERTIFICATE OF PUBLISHING
We're proud to present this certificate of publishing to
Abdul Waheed
for successfully publishing
GRIEF
on 20-01-2023
"A writer's life and work are not a gift to mankind; they're a necessity"~ Toni Morrison

Dedication

This book is dedicated to the memory of my late father Haji Ubairdur Rahman (Munna) and younger brother Abdul Hameed. May God (Allah) give peace to his soul.

Amen

Table of contents

Preface

In today's run-of-the-mill life, there is definitely some sorrow near every human being, although this sorrow has been going on since ancient times, which remains with the human being, be it small or big sorrow. To know a little about this, the thoughts of Gautam Buddha have been displayed as he has discussed in detail about suffering. You also read this book and if there is any incomplete knowledge about sorrow, then inform it. Yours - Abdul Waheed Barabanki, UP, India.

Date-22/11/2022

Sadness (SAD)

Biography of Gautam Buddha

The name of Gautam Buddha, the founder of Buddhism, was Siddhartha and the name of his dynasty was Gautam. He was born in 566 AD. Poo I was born in a Kshatriya Rajkul named Shakya, in a village named Lumbini in the Terai near the Indo-Nepal border. His father's name was King Suddhodana and mother's name was Mayadevi. The name of the capital of his father's republic was Kapilavastu. Seven days after the birth of Siddhartha, his mother died. He was brought up by his aunt. His childhood and youth passed in very happy and royal splendor. He was married to a very beautiful princess named Yashodhara, from whom he had a son named Rahul. Even after getting so much happiness, Siddhartha was not satisfied with his life. Much of his time was spent in deep contemplation and thinking. Inspite of having a lot of arrangements for enjoyment and entertainment, his mind was not happy with these, one day Siddhartha left the palace for a walk. While sitting in the chariot, he saw some such forms of reality of human life which made his mind very impressed and restless. A very old and dilapidated man, whose teeth were broken due to old age, his hair was gray and his waist was bent and doubled, with the help of a stick, he was walking slowly trembling. Then he saw an extremely emaciated patient who was moaning in a diseased state. Then saw a hearse of a dead body leaving and people mourning, crying and beating their chests going behind it. Then he had a vision of a monk in a calm and serious posture, who was walking around surrounded by the sorrows of the world with a begging bowl in his hand. These four scenes created a great upheaval in his mind and a revolution in his thoughts. Why does man get sick, why does he suffer, why does he grow old and why does he die?

He became obsessed with knowing the answers to these questions. Being imprisoned in the royal splendor of the palace, he had no idea of these states of man. The more Siddhartha looked at these stages of human life, the more his anxiety increased. In the end, in order to put an end to this distraction, he determined to find a way to remove the sufferings of the world by renouncing the royal pleasures. He always used to think about the world full of sorrows. Sadness, seriousness and contemplation had become the permanent instincts of his life. Even the attachment to the household could not remove his disenchantment with worldly luxuries and pleasures. At last, at the age of 21, in the stillness of one night, leaving his son Rahul and his wife to sleep, renouncing all pleasures, he came out of the palace with his charioteer. This incident in his life is known as Mahabhinishkraman and after traveling overnight he came outside the limits of his kingdom and cut his hair with a sharp saber. Taking off his ornaments, he gave them to the charioteer and sent him back with the horse. Then changed his clothes from a villager and assumed the form of a monk. In this way, after taking sannyas, for about six years he wandered to saints, sages, ascetics, scholars and pundits in search of ways to gain knowledge and remove worldly sorrows.He got disappointment in all these efforts. Then he did severe penance for six years with his five companions at a place called Uruvela in a dense forest near Gaya city of Bihar province. As a result of this austerity, his body remained just a bone. Even then he did not get knowledge. Leaving the path of harsh penance, he now started thinking about the middle path. The middle path is neither the path of excessive attachment to pleasures nor the adoption of sleeplessness, starvation, austerity, severe self-torture, etc. The middle path between these two extremist paths is considered to be the middle path. His five companions left him thinking that he had lost his penance. At that time, when he was thinking about his life sitting under a Peepal tree, he suddenly got enlightenment. His inner soul got illuminated by this divine light of knowledge.

Because of this attainment of truth-knowledge or 'realization', Prince Siddhartha was called 'Buddha', and became famous among the people as Gautam Buddha. The Peepal tree under which the prince attained 'enlightenment' while sitting in the Vichar Magra Mudra, became famous as the Bodhi tree. In course of time, this tree became worshipable for the followers of Buddhism.

Gautam Buddha wanted to give the message of knowledge to the whole world. For this, he started campaigning by traveling. First of all, he came to a place called Sarnath near Varanasi and gave his first religious sermon there at Mrigkunj place. There he got the opportunity to meet his old companions again, who became his disciples after listening to his teachings. This very first sermon is of great importance in Buddhism. Gautam Buddha taught to adopt the middle path. The place near Gaya where he attained self-enlightenment and was called Buddha, became famous as Bodh Gaya and became a place of pilgrimage for Buddhists. Similarly Sarnath where he made the first five disciples and his birth place Lumbini also became sacred pilgrimage sites for Buddhists and Buddhist followers from far off countries come to visit these places. He gave the message of adopting the eight-fold path for suffering, their causes and remedies. A lot of emphasis was laid on non-violence. He opposed rituals and animal sacrifice.Gautam Buddha went to Rajgriha from Sarnath while preaching. There he made many scholars his disciples and there Magadha-King Bimbasar also took initiation into Buddhism. He propagated his message in Pali, the simple spoken language of the common people. The doors of Buddhism were open to all kinds of people. Be it a Brahmin or a Shudra, a sinner or a Chandal, a woman or a man, a householder or a celibate, Buddhism accepted people of all classes. In Buddhism, there was no discrimination between Varnashram Dharma, high and low, rich and poor. The number of followers of Buddhism started increasing rapidly. Big kings, rich moneylenders and scholars started becoming his disciples. As a result, the Buddhist Sangha was established in which not only monks but also nuns were allowed membership.   In   this   way,   Gautam   Buddha   attained 'Mahaparinirvana' by leaving his body at the age of 80 in Kushinagar i.e. Kasia under present-day Gorakhpur district in Uttar Pradesh by preaching religion continuously for 44 years. After death, eight castes divided the ashes of his body among themselves and built different stupas on them. A colossal statue of him was erected in Kushinagar at the spot where he attained Nirvana. This idol is still present today. Kushinagar is a very sacred pilgrimage place for Buddhists.

Context – Major Religions of the World

Buddha's Teachings

Buddha's principles and teachings were simple and practical, he emphasized on moral life and virtue and told that the debate related to soul-divine-spirit is never helpful in the moral progress of man. He declared this world as mortal, eternal and full of sorrow and told mankind the way to get rid of this all-pervading sorrow. The four noble truths are famous in his teachings. these are

1. Sorrow There is sorrow everywhere in the world. Birth, death, old age and disease are sorrows, dear - separation, unpleasant - coincidence and not getting the desired thing is also sorrow. All the creatures of the world are suffering from these miseries.

2. The Community of Sorrows (The Cause of Sorrow) The cause of this world wide sorrow is craving or 'loneliness'. Due to the insatiable craving for worldly pleasures, man gets trapped in the bondage of sorrows. Due to this craving ego, affection, attachment-hatred etc. sorrows arise.

3. Sorrow - Opposition or prevention of sorrow is possible only by the destruction of unquenchable craving or lust. Traffic and other sorrows can be destroyed only after the end of all cravings. The name of the state of freedom from rebirth and other sorrows is 'Nirvana'.

4. Sorrow Nirodhgamini Pratipada This sorrow can be resisted only by following the eightfold path. Prayers, sacrifices, chanting of Veda-mantras and penance are all futile for this. The following are the eight things in the eightfold path

1. Right vision – Right faith and right perspective is the only right vision. By which good and bad deeds are identified.

2- Right resolution Strong thoughts are right resolution.

3. Right speech is true and dear words are right speech. 4- Right deeds are right actions. 5- Right livelihood: The only way to live is the right livelihood.

6- Right exercise: The name of pure and judicious efforts is right exercise. It includes sense-restraint and high thoughts.

7. Samyak Smriti – Be aware of the feelings of the conscious about every ritual and effort of the human body. Recognizing the attachment and aversion of the mind, do all the work with discretion and caution, this is the right memory.

8–. Samyak Samadhi – The stillness of the mind and the meditative state is called Samyak Samadhi. This gives inner peace and joy.

This eightfold path is the famous middle path of Buddha, 'Majjhima Patipada' seen by Tathagat. This is the middle path between bodily pleasures and physical suffering caused by austerity, which could be followed even by householders who did not take Pravjya. In this extreme has been opposed. One can give peace of mind by living a moral life.Buddha laid a lot of emphasis on moral life in his teachings. Virtue, love, truth, generosity, obedience to parents, devotion to teachers, prohibition of alcohol, compassion and charity had a special place in his moral teachings. It was necessary for the monks of the Buddhist Sangha to follow the purity of Mansa-Vacha-Karma to attain Nirvana. He preached ten precepts for monks, of which the first five were compulsory for householders or ordinary worshippers. These are- 1. Non-violence, 2. Truth, 3. Asteya (non-stealing), 4. Renunciation of non-violence, 5. Brahmacharya, 6. Sacrifice of dance-song, 7. Sacrifice of fragrant substances, garlands, 8. Sacrifice of Akal Bhojal, 9. Sacrifice of soft bed, 10. Sacrifice of Kamini Kanchan.

Buddha accepted rebirth in his philosophy. He declared that a man gets good or bad birth as a result of his deeds. Despite not believing in God and soul, Buddha believed in reincarnation. According to him, rebirth is not of the soul, but of the impermanent ego. When a man's lust, which is the mother of renunciation and affection, is destroyed, then he becomes free from the bondage of rebirth. Just as a lamp gets extinguished by itself when oil and wick are burnt, in the same way, by the destruction of lust and ego, a man gets freedom from the bondage of karma and attains ultimate peace, which is called 'Nirvana'. Nirvana is the ultimate goal of Buddhism. By its attainment one gets relief from all sufferings, end of the attachment of life and freedom from the bondage of rebirth. This is the state of supreme peace. Non-violence and compassion also have an important place in Buddha's teachings, but the importance given to the spirit of non-violence in Jainism is not in Buddha's teachings. Kindness and love towards all living beings was necessary in his view, but at the same time he also allowed meat-eating.He rejected the principle of authenticity and infallibility of the Vedas. He was strongly opposed to Vedic rituals, complex yagya-practice and harsh sacrifice. He condemned tantra-mantra and superstitions and opposed the inequality prevalent in the society due to caste system. Refused to accept the supremacy of Brahmins. He did not give any place to priesthood, penance, yagya and caste system in his religion. The door of his religion was open to all castes and classes. In this way, his teachings proved helpful in bringing not only religious revolution, but also social revolution.

Reference - History of Ancient Civilizations of the World, Bihar Hindi Granth Academy.

last time

Buddha left his body at the age of 80; But even before this, his religion had established great strength and firmness in the Buddha 50 worlds. In the end, Buddha once again preached to the disciples and explained the essence of religion and ordered them to be firm in their religion. Buddha said - "If a man makes up his mind that he has faith in the Buddha, the Sangha and the Dharma, then he is liberated." Moolmantra was done. The Lord said with joy, "O joy! You are the light unto yourself. After me, do not take refuge in any other external protector, be firm in the truth like a protector. "When Ananda started crying and repenting holding a peg in Bihar knowing that the time of Nirvana of Buddha was near, then Buddha called him to him and said --" Ananda! Don't be sad now. Didn't I tell you that it is natural that loved ones get separated. The thing that was born, destruction is in it. How is it possible that you should not perish because you have shown affection towards me. Your love never decreased. You stick to your industry. You will also become free from evil and will attain Nirvana. I am not and will not be the last Buddha. As long as my disciples, I, the first Buddha in the world, follow the Dharma with purity, the promotion of Dharma will continue.

Reference - Vishwa Dharma Darshan, Bihar National Language Council.

buddhist philosophy

After the Mahaparinirvana of Gautama Buddha, different sects of Buddhism have appeared, but they all share many principles.

apparent derivative

The principle of Pratityasamutpada states that any event exists only because of other events in a complex cause-effect web. For the living beings, it means the cycle of infinite samsara according to karma and vipaka (results of karma). Because everything is impermanent and aatman (without soul), nothing truly exists. Every event is basically zero. However, humans, who have the power of knowledge, can attain nirvana by giving up craving, which is the cause of suffering, and by converting the energy wasted in craving into knowledge and meditation. A life without craving is possible only through Vipassana. In today's era, the apparent product should disappear somewhere from the society.

Transcendentalism

Everything in this world is transient and mortal. Nothing is permanent. But it is different from Vedic opinion.
anathema

The meaning of soul is 'I'. But, beings are made of body and mind, which have no permanence. Changes happen every moment. Therefore, there is no permanent thing called 'I' ie soul. What people think of as soul is a continuous flow of consciousness. The mind has taken the place of the soul.

atheism

Buddha has told how the world was created in the Brahma-Jaal thread. Creation and destruction of the universe happen again and again. God or Mahabrahma does not create the universe because the world runs on the principle of Pratityasamutpada i.e. the principle of action. According to Lord Buddha, Karma is responsible for the sorrows and happiness of human beings, not God or Mahabrahma. But elsewhere the Buddha has called the Supreme Truth indescribable.

nihilism
Emptiness is the main philosophy of Mahayana Buddhism.
realism
Buddhism does not mean pessimism. Sadness does not mean pessimism, but relativism and realism. Buddha, Dhamma and Sangha are the three gems of Buddhism. Monks, nuns, upasakas and upasikas are the four components of the Sangha.
Bodhisatva

The one who fully observes the ten perfections is called a Bodhisattva. Bodhisattvas are called "Buddhas" when they attain the ten forces or lands (Mudita, Vimala, Dipti, Archishmati, Sudurjaya, Abhimukhi, Durangama, Achal, Sadhumati, Dhamma-megha). Becoming a Buddha is the culmination of a bodhisattva's life. This recognition is named Bodhi (enlightenment). Buddha Shakyamuni is said to be the only Buddha -- There were many before him and there will be more in the future. He said that anyone can become a Buddha if he attains Bodhisattva by fully following the Ten Perfections and after Bodhisattva attains the Ten Forces or Lands. The ultimate goal of Buddhism is the end of suffering from the entire human society. "I teach only one substance – there is suffering, the cause of suffering, the cessation of suffering, and the path to the cessation of suffering" (Buddha). Followers of Buddhism try to get rid of ignorance and sorrow and attain nirvana by following the eightfold path and living according to the no.

There are innumerable places in ancient Buddhist literature where these have been explained again and again in more and more detail and in different ways. If we study the Four Noble Truths with the help of these references and clarifications, we get a fairly satisfactory, profoundly correct account of the Buddha's fundamental teachings according to these original texts. These are the four universal truths:

1 - Dukkha (sorrow),

2- Samudaya, that is, the origin of sorrow or its origin,

3-Prevention, prevention of sorrow means its end, 4-- Magga, (path) cessation of sorrow or prevention Gamini Pratipada (Patipada).

Grief

The first noble truth (dukkha ariyasachcha) is "suffering is the noblest truth", life according to Buddhists is nothing but pain and suffering. But Buddhism is neither pessimistic nor utopian or fatalistic. because its approach to life and the world is realistic. It sees things in their objective (Yatha Bhootam) form. It neither gives you false solace nor overshadows and afflicts you with many kinds of imaginary fears and sins. It Tells you decisively and objectively what you are? And what is the world around you? What is your relation to the world-cycle? A doctor may seriously exaggerate a disease and tell the body to be cured. Give up Prasha altogether. The second doctor, thus deceiving the patient by giving false consolation, ignorantly declares that there is no disease and no treatment is needed. You can call the first doctor a pessimist and the second an optimist. Both the doctors are equally terrible. But the third doctor correctly diagnoses the symptoms of the disease, understands the cause and nature of the disease, clearly sees that the disease can be cured and courageously gives complete treatment and saves the patient. Lord Buddha is like this third type of doctor. He is the intelligent and scientific physician (Bhishak or Bhaishajya-guru) of Bhava-diseases. , As the First Noble Truth—the word "dukkha," which refers to the Buddha's view of life and the world, has a more profound philosophical meaning and a far wider sense. It is accepted that the word "dukkha" as the first objective truth clearly conveys the simple meaning of "suffering" but along with it serious ideas like 'incompleteness', 'impermanence', 'emptiness', 'exhaustibility' ' are also included. Therefore, it is difficult to find a single word in whose meaning the whole concept of the word dukkha as the first noble truth can be expressed.

Lord Buddha does not deny the pleasures of life when he says that there is sorrow. On the contrary, they accept different states of happiness, both material and spiritual, for laymen - householders as well as monks. Like the happiness of household life, the happiness of sense-born pleasure and the happiness born of renunciation of everything, the happiness of attachment and the happiness of detachment, physical happiness and mental happiness etc. But all these are included in sorrow. It is "suffering", not because it is 'suffering' in the ordinary sense of the word, but because "all that is temporary and impermanent is dukkha (yadanvam tamam dukkham).

2- Dukh Samudya - The root cause of sorrow

The second dharma satya is the origin or root cause of suffering (dukhasamudaya dhariyas). The well-known and well-known definition of this second primal truth, as found at numerous places in the original texts, is as follows: "It is craving (lipsa, lalasa, tamha) that is the cause of rebirth and rebirth (ponobhavika), and One who is bound by lustful greed (nandirag sahgata) and who takes pleasure again and again in this and sometimes in that (tavatvabhinandini), yaya (1) craving for five sense pleasures (kama-tanha), (2) eternal vision or Attachment to existence, man's yearning for re-birth and status (bhava-tanha), (3) yearning for the vision of no re-birth (vibhava-tanha) leads man to accept the past unattainable life and indulge in arbitrary enjoyment. luxuries. This craving, aspiration, greed, longing expresses itself in various forms. It is the reason for the origin of all kinds of sorrows and the re-birth of man. But it should not be considered as the first reason, because According to Buddhism, nothing is primary, everything is relative and other is dependent.   Each is dependent for its rise (community) on something else, which is sensation.(pain) is;   And the rise of sensation-perception is dependent on contact (phass), and so on and so forth the cycle goes on, which is called hetu-pratyaya-vada, (pratyaya samutpada, paticcha samuppada). Pratityasamutpada is the theory of the origin of impermanent action from impermanent causes. This principle is the backbone of Buddhism. Without going into details, it is necessary to say that it is sufficient to remember that the center of craving is our ignorance and the false conception of the ego as our self that arises from it.

Thus craving is not the first and only reason for the rise of unhappiness. But it is the most obvious and immediate cause, the "principal cause" and the "pervading subject". Therefore, at some places in the original Pali texts, in addition to tava, trishna, which is always given the first place, other defilements and impurities (kilesa, sasavadhamma) are also included in the definitions of the causes of the origin of sorrow in the Samudaya Granth. For our discussion it is necessary to know in this limited space that we should remember that this center of craving is supposed to be ours.

Here the word Tushna does not mean only the desire for sense-pleasures, wealth and power and the desire for them, but also includes the desire and desire for feelings and objects, attitudes, opinions, principles, beliefs and beliefs (Dhammatva). . According to the Buddha's interpretation, all the disturbances and conflicts in the world, from small personal family disputes to fierce wars between nations and countries, are due to this selfish motive.From this point of view, the root cause of all economic, political and social problems is this selfish greed. Big politicians who try to settle international disputes and talk of war and peace only in the literal and political sense. I talk superficially, talk superficially and do not go to the depth of the real root of the problem. As Lord Buddha said to Ratthapala "This world lives in want and longing and remains a slave of "craving". (Tanhadaso).

3-- Nirodh: "The Cessation of Suffering"

The third shrayam (best) truth is called the noble truth of the end of sorrow. (Dukkhanirodha - Ariyasachcha), this is "Nibban", which is highly regarded as the Sanskrit word "Nirvana". To eliminate sorrow completely, the root cause of sorrow, ie craving, has to be destroyed, as we have seen earlier. Therefore, Nirvana is also called Tahkkhay "Destruction of craving". For this now you will say what is Nirvana? Now let us consider some of the definitions and interpretations of nirvana as found in the original Pali texts "It is the complete cessation of craving (tanha), leaving it, giving it up, getting rid of it, separation from it. To remain calm, to stabilize all bound things, to give up all impurity, to destroy craving, to stop detachment, to stop desires, this is Nivvan (Nirvana). Bhikkhus, this is the complete annihilation of desires (ragakkhayo, ragakshaya), the complete annihilation of hatred (domakkhayo, dveshakshaya), the destruction of attachment (mohakkhayo, mohakshaya). O monks! This is what is called nirvana. Tahkkhyo) is the nivban. O bhikkhus, of all things with or without bondage, detachment is the highest. This means -To get rid of ego, to destroy craving, to root out attachment, to end the continuity of births, the full name of craving, to be free from attachment, to end desires, this is Nibbaan. A Parivrajaka asked a direct question to Saripuva, the chief disciple of the Buddha, 'What is Nibyana? ' Saripura's answer is clear destruction of desire, complete cessation of craving, destruction of attachment. The

Buddha's statement in relation to the Nibyana is - "Bhikshusro. He is the unborn, the unborn, the inferior community. If there were no Prajata, Abhuta, and unrecognizable arising situation, then it is not possible to get rid of the Jata, Bhuta, and Pratya arising situation." The four elements of solidity, fluidity, heat and motion have no place in the state, neither death nor birth, nor sense objects are found. To say that nirvana is negative or positive is not correct. The feelings of negativism and positivity are relative and come in the range of dualism. These beliefs cannot be applied to Nirvana (Absolute Truth), because it is beyond duality and relativity.

4 - **Magga: Way or way**

Chauya Arya Satya is the way or remedy to prevent (nirodh) suffering (dukkha nirodhagamini patipada - ariya satcha). This is the middle path (Majjhima Patida). so called, because it avoids both ends, counterarguments: one end is the pursuit of pleasure through sense pleasures, which is the "low, common, unprofitable and commoner's way", the other means or path to afflict oneself with various types of austerities, which are 'painful, unfit and unprofitable'. Having tried both these extremes himself, and finding them futile, the Buddha through his personal experience invented the 'middle way', which Provides vision and knowledge, which leads to peace, insight, nirvana. This middle path is commonly called the 'Arya Ashtangik Marg' (Ariya-Atungik Magga), because it is made up of Graha categories or limbs:

1 - Right view (Sammaditthi)

2- Right Thought (Samma Sankappa)

3- Samyak Vacha (Samma Vacha)

4 - Right action (Samma Kammant)

5- Right livelihood (samma ajiva)

6- Right effort (Samma exercise)

7 -- Right memory (samma sati) -

8- Right concentration (Samma Samadhi)

In fact, the entire teaching of the Buddha, which he himself practiced for 45 years of his life, represents this path. He has explained different people in different ways and in different words according to their level of spiritual development and their ability to understand and follow themselves. The essence of thousands of discourses scattered in Buddhist scriptures is found in Arya Ashtangik Marg only. It should not be thought that this path should be followed one by one by the eight categories or divisions of body behavior according to the number in which they are ordinarily given in the above list. Rather, they should be developed almost simultaneously as far as possible according to the capacity of each individual. They are related to each other and each part helps in the development of the other part. (The purpose of these eight elements is to enhance and bring to perfection the three essentials of Buddhist education and discipline, namely (a) seal (virtue), (b) Samadhi (discipline of the mind) and (c) Panja (discipline) Prajna. To understand the eight limbs of the Shrataeva path coherently and thoroughly, it will be more helpful if they are classified and clarified under these three headings. The construction of the seal (virtue) is based on a broad sense of friendship and compassion for all beings, which is the foundation of the Buddha's teaching. The Buddha, because of his compassion for the world, did not limit his teachings to any specific individual or community. Not for the benefit, but for the benefit of many, for the happiness of many (Bahujan Hitaya, Bahujan Sukhaya, Lokanukampaya).

According to Buddhism, in order to attain perfection, one must develop two qualities equally, 'compassion' on the one hand and 'prudence' (panja) on the other. Here 'karuna' refers to love, kindness, tolerance and other such emotional qualities or qualities of the heart, while 'pragya' or prudence refers to the intellectual side or mental qualities. If one develops only emotional qualities by neglecting intellectual qualities, he will become a good-hearted (good-hearted) fool, whereas if one develops only intellectual qualities by neglecting the emotional side, the person may become harsh without caring for others. Will become an intelligent creature with a heart. Therefore, in order to become a complete human being, it is necessary for a person to develop both the sides equally. This is the aim of the Buddhist way of life. In this prudence and compassion are inextricably linked. Now, modesty is virtue or moral conduct. It includes three elements of the Noble Eightfold Path: namely, right speech, right action and right prajeev. Meaning of

Samyak Vacha (1) Refraining from speaking untruth (2) Pisuna Vacha Abstaining from speaking evil and slander behind the back, doing such things that create hatred, enmity, division and disharmony between individuals or groups of people.

3) Farusa Vacha is abstinence from speaking bitter, dear, rude, hateful and abusive words and (4) Samphapatap is abstinence from useless, empty and foolish chatter and blasphemy. When one refrains from these inappropriate and harmful things of behaviour, it naturally becomes necessary for him to speak the truth. It becomes necessary to use such words, which are friendly and generous, pleasant and polite, meaningful and useful. One should not speak carelessly, the conversation should be done at the appropriate time and place. If a person cannot say anything useful, he should resort to "Arya (Elegant) Mon". The purpose of Sampark Karma is to inculcate moral, dignified, and peaceful conduct. This is to alert us that we should refrain from killing animals, stealing, dishonest actions (falsehood) and illegal work. It is also that we should help others to lead a peaceful and dignified life in a proper way. Right livelihood means that one should abstain from earning one's livelihood by such occupations as may cause harm to others, such as shrayudh and deadly weapons, intoxicating drinks, poison, for killing, treachery towards animals. Fraudulent business One should earn his livelihood by doing such a business, which is prestigious, unblemished and free from the fault of harming other

persons. These three parts of the Eightfold Path (right speech, right action and right living) are the virtues related to modesty.

It should be understood that the aim of Buddhist ideals and ethical conduct is to develop a happy and harmonious life for both the individual and society. This ethical conduct is considered the indispensable basis for all higher spiritual attainments. No spiritual development is possible without this moral foundation. Next comes the discipline of the mind, which includes the other three parts of the Noble Eightfold Path, namely, right exercise (effort), right memory (or mental concentration) and right samadhi. Right exercise means (1) preventing the emergence of faulty and conflicting mental states, and (2) getting rid of such faulty and disordered states that have already arisen in one's mind, and (3) bringing about happy and healthy mental states that have hitherto been have not yet arisen, for their emergence, and (4) for the development and fulfilment of pre-existing benevolent and benevolent mental states in man, Bajwati desire is to wish. (2) Sensation (Vedana) or Anubhuti (3) Activities of the mind (Chitta) and (4) Thoughts, thoughts (Dhamma) Perceptions and effort in relation to objects is to remain alert and meditative. In the 'Satipathana Sutta' (The Sutra to Steady Vigilance) these four forms of government or meditation of the mind are discussed in detail. The third and final element of disciplining the mind or chitta is samyak samadhi, in which, as in the fourth state of transcendental meditation, all sensations, of pleasure and pain, joy and sadness, cease and only pure equanimity and consciousness remain. Stays here . By this the mind or chitta is trained and disciplined and it is developed by right exercise, right memory and right meditation.

The remaining two parts, ie right intention and discretion, are awakened. From this point of view, right resolution or right thought is indicative of selfless sacrifice or disinterest, love and friendship for all beings and non-violence. It is to be noted here and it is important that the feelings of selfless detachment, love and minister and non-violence have been subsumed in favor of discretion. It becomes clear from this. that Prajna (prudence) is possessed of these noble qualities and that all thoughts of selfish desires, ill-will, hatred and violence in all spheres of life, whether personal, social or political, and in any sphere, are prudence the result is . Right vision or right understanding is the understanding of things as they are, and these are the four noble truths, which interpret things as they really are. Therefore, right vision ultimately leads to the realization of the four noble truths. This right vision is the highest intelligence, which sees the ultimate reality. According to Buddhism, there are two types of perception or wisdom. Ordinarily we call it wisdom, that knowledge, accumulated memory, is to be grasped by the intellect according to a given description. This is "knowing the truth" dharmat "anubodh" or other things. It is not very deep. Real deep understanding Understanding with subtle intelligence (prativedh, pativedh), is called seeing the substance in its real form, without name or label. This restriction, the penetrating vision of the subtle intelligence, is possible only then. When the mind is free from all disorders and has been fully developed through meditation. From this brief description of the "way" one can see that it is a way of life for every individual to follow, practice and grow. This path of body, speech and mind; Self-discipline, self-development and self-purification Of This path leads to complete liberation, happiness and peace through the realization of the essential reality (factuity) and through moral, spiritual and intellectual perfection. Buddhists have simple and elegant customs and ceremonies on religious occasions. They have nothing to do with the real religious path. But these practices and ceremonies have their own importance in order to satisfy some religious feelings and needs and to gradually increase such people who have been able to progress relatively little on the path of religion. There are four essential acts we have to do in relation to the Four Noble Truths: The first Noble Truth is 'suffering', the nature of life, its sufferings, its sadness and joy, its incompleteness and dissatisfaction, its impermanence and all. Our task in this regard is to understand it clearly and completely as a fact (parigyaya). The second noble truth is the emergence of unhappiness, which is desire, "trishna", with all the calamitous desires, faults and impurities attached to it. Merely understanding this fact is not enough. Here our task is to remove it, to eliminate it, to destroy it and to destroy it completely (pahattabb). The third step is truth, the cessation of suffering, and nirvana, the ultimate truth, the ultimate reality. Here our act is to understand it well (sandikabya) and do Dhanubhav. The fourth is often the path of Satya Nirvana Sadhna. Mere knowledge of this path or aspect, no matter how complete it is, is not enough. In this regard, our action is to follow and be engaged in this spiritual practice. As much as the philosophy of Lord Buddha is humane and spiritual, to that extent his behavior is also egalitarian and humane. In the end, it seems appropriate to discuss something in that regard in brief. Lord Buddha in the common sense Whether the ideology of Lord Buddha should be called religion or better than human spiritualism, this is a matter to be considered. But seeing Lord Buddha in that category, Lord Buddha is the only religion promoter who can tell that he is a human being. Lord Buddha has not told himself whether he is an incarnation of God or has been sent by God. Lord Buddha has not even told himself to be inspired by any divine power. He has attained Buddhahood in this human body through human intelligence. Lord Buddha was the one who told this fact. Not only this, only human beings can attain enlightenment and this power is present in every human being. In order to attain the knowledge of Buddha, qualities like virya, adhishthana, faith, wisdom etc. are required. In Buddhists, this quality has been described as ten perfections. In spite of being such a human being, Lord Buddha was surprisingly a superior human being. According to Buddhism, man is the only answer and the best. There is no external divine power or divine man to decide his future. Man is his own master, he is his own speed. Be your refuge, don't seek refuge in others. In the Dhammapada, and the Mahaparinirvana Sutra, Lord Buddha has given a clear order to his disciples that man has the power to free himself from all bondages by the power of his intelligence and enthusiasm and the command to achieve his upliftment and liberation by his own efforts is also very important. In words Lord Buddha gave to his disciples. You have to work, if Lord Buddha is called Raksha, then it is in the sense that he had shown us the path of Nirvana i.e. freedom from sorrow. But achieving Nirvana by following that path is our own task, Tathagat is just a guide. Tathagata left his disciples free because each person is responsible for himself. In the Mahaparinirvana Sutra, the Lord has said, "Mananda! I have preached the Dharma from within, not from the outside. Yananda! There is no Pacharya Mushti (mystery) of the Tathagat in Dharma. He must respect me for my purpose! Say something for the Sangha. Ananda Tathagat has nothing to say. Without realizing the truth as one's own, one is afflicted by the merciful blessings received by some divine power for obedient virtues. Can't get freedom from this. Hence man needs this freedom. Once Tathagat Kosala had come to a corporation named Keshput (Kesputta). The people of this corporation were known by the name "Kalam". Hearing this, Kalam, a resident of Keshput, went to the place where God was and said: "Bhante! Some Shraman-Brahmin come to Keshputra, they publish their own opinion, shine, condemn other's opinion. Disrespect , despise, Bhante! Who among you Shraman Brahmins told the truth and who lied? Tathagat answered this question in the following form, which is well-known in the history of religions, "Kalamo! It is okay for you to doubt, to be in doubt. It is okay, because you are confused about doubting."

Kalamo! You people don't accept any opinion because it comes from Shruti, don't accept it because it is traditional, don't accept it because it has been doing so, don't accept it because it matches with the scriptures, don't accept it even from justice Don't accept even if you are of a dhakar type, don't accept even if you like it, don't accept with an attractive personality and accept that this Shraman is our worshipper. Now Kalam |You people take paddy yourself, things are flawed, these things are beneficial and sad, then the work is yours (bad), you should not accept this! You people don't accept anything because it comes from Shruti, don't accept it because of being traditional, don't accept that they have been doing like this. Don't accept that religion matches with scriptures, don't accept even by logic, don't accept even by justice, don't accept even by being beautiful, don't accept even by liking, don't accept because of attractive personality Accept and don't accept that this Shraman is our worshipper. When the columns! You people know for yourself that these things are efficient, these things are innocent, these things are praised by the knowledgeable, then you people should roam free from them. The Lord said -- "The bhikshutra-disputer bhikkhus should inform about the Tathagat in relation to the dharmas (=things) that can be known by the eye-source -- which the eye-source is the vijable malindharma (=paap), that (Is this) Tathagata's, or not? Examining him (when) he sees that - eye source cognizable malin dharma is not in Tathagata. --- then further investigates which eye source -- cognizable (= sin and virtue mixed) Dharma, is it in Tathagata or not? -Vyati-Mitra Dharma is not in Tathagata. Then he further investigates -- the eye which is srota = cognizable avadat (=pure) dharma (=virtue), is in Tathagata Or not ?

According to the teaching of Tathagat, this vichikichha (doubt) is one of the Panchni Varanas that hinder spiritual progress, that is, for all kinds of progress, for true philosophy. But doubting is not a sin. There is no list of policies regarding the devotion of Shravakas in Buddhism. In the same way, in the religious world in the general popular sense, the festival in which sin is taken, in that sense no "sin" Also not in Buddhism. All the skilled means dush varikhtathas and have wrong vision (Mithya Drishti). As long as there is doubt, grudge, upheaval, there is no growth, progress in intelligence, not knowing the origin (bhavijja). In the same way, until it is not understood clearly, the curiosity does not go away, this is also an undisputed truth. If you want progress in the future, then it is necessary to get rid of doubts and doubts. Right vision is necessary to be free from doubt.

Reference - The Way of Peace

Theory

Gautam Buddha did not try to establish any new religion or sect by himself. Neither did he discuss about religious principles and customs nor about rules and regulations. He only indicated towards a new path of life. By following this path of virtues, one can get freedom from the bondage of life and death. The basis of his teachings is the purity of soul, work and conduct. They rejected the authenticity and apaurusheyata (i.e. created by God) of the Vedas. Condemned the violent tendencies like animal-sacrifice in Yagyas and strongly opposed meaningless religious methods and rituals. Challenged the caste system and the supremacy of Brahmins. Expressed doubt in the existence of God who created the world. He did not get involved in the quarrels between the soul and the Supreme Soul. According to him personal labor and virtuous life are most important for his own development. The virtuous and virtuous path that he has suggested is a set of practical, moral qualities. He is prudent. Therefore Buddhism was more of a social revolution than a religious revolution. Buddha's Teachings

Gautama Buddha preached the following Four Noble Truths: 1. There is suffering in this world, 2. This suffering has a cause, 3. This cause is desire or lust, 4. This sorrow can be removed by destroying the lust, to avoid bondage or to end sorrows, man should follow the eightfold path. The following eight things are included in this eight-fold path: 1. Right view, 2. Right thought, 3. Right speech, 4. Right action, 5. Right living, 6. Right effort, 7. Right memory and 8. Right Samadhi.

Buddha emphasized on the simplicity of life. According to him, there is no importance of high-low feeling in the society. He said that it is not necessary for a person to be born in a high caste to lead a pious life. That's why he made all those people members of the Buddhist Sangha without discrimination who wanted to become members of the Sangha. Buddha gave his teachings in the language of the common people. That's why they became very popular.

Both Buddha and Mahavira believed in these principles. But there is also a great difference between the teachings of Buddha and Mahavira. Buddha emphasized the middle path. According to him, in order to lead a pious life, one should avoid both extremes. He should neither do harsh penance nor should he completely indulge in lust for the attainment of worldly pleasures. Keep in mind that Lord Mahavir has given more emphasis on harsh penance and physical torture. Like Mahavira, Buddha also preached non-violence.

Reference - Pustak Mahal, Delhi.

Tafsir of the Holy Qur'an
Tafsir ibne kathir

Surah Al kahf 18, ayat 6

Do not feel sorry because the Idolators do not believe

Allah consoles His Messenger for his sorrow over the idolators because they would not believe and keep away from him.

He also said:

فَلَ تَذْهَبْ نَفْسُكَ عَلَيْهِمْ حَسَرَتٍ

So destroy not yourself in sorrow for them. (35:8)

وَلَا تَحْزَنْ عَلَيْهِمْ

And grieve not over them. (16:127)

لَعَلَّكَ بَـخِعٌ نَّفْسَكَ أَلاَّ يَكُونُواْ مُوْمِنِينَ

It may be that you are going to kill yourself with grief, that they do not become believers. (26:3)

meaning, maybe you will destroy yourself with your grief over them.

Allah says:

فَلَعَلَّكَ بَاخِعٌ نَّفْسَكَ عَلَى اثَارِهِمْ إِن لَّمْ يُوْمِنُوا بِهَذَا الْحَدِيثِ

Perhaps, you would kill yourself in grief, over their footsteps, because they believe not in this narration.

meaning the Qur'an.

أَسَفًا

in grief.

Allah is saying, 'do not destroy yourself with regret.'

Qatadah said:

"killing yourself with anger and grief over them."

Mujahid said:

"with anxiety."

These are synonymous, so the meaning is:
'Do not feel sorry for them, just convey the Message of Allah to them. Whoever goes the right way, then he goes the right way only for the benefit of himself. And whoever goes astray, then he strays at his own loss, so do not destroy yourself in sorrow for them.'
This World is the Place of Trial

Then Allah tells us that He has made this world a temporary abode, adorned with transient beauty, and He made it a place of trial, not a place of settlement. So He says:

$$\text{إِنَّا جَعَلْنَا مَا عَلَى الأَرْضِ زِينَةً لَّهَا لِنَبْلُوَهُمْ أَيُّهُمْ أَحْسَنُ عَمَلً}$$

Tafsir jalallain

Yet it may be that you will consume, destroy, yourself in their wake -- following [your being with] them, that is, after they have left you -- if they should not believe in this discourse, [in this] Qur'n, out of grief, out of rage and anguish on your part, because of your eagerness that they believe (asafan, 'out of grief', is in the accusative because it functions as an object denoting reason).

Tafsir as Sadi

Surah Al baqra 2, ayat 155

Allah, the Exalted and Exalted, informed that He tests His servants through hardships and tribulations, so that the difference between the truthful and the false, the patient and the impatient, becomes clear. In the case of His servants, this is the Sunnah of Allah, the Exalted, because if the believers always enjoy prosperity and never face hardships, then corruption will occur, and the wisdom of Allah requires that the people of the good and the people of the evil. Separate from me. This is the benefit of trial. This does not make the faith of the believers disappear that has been given to them, nor does the trial turn them away from the religion, Allah does not destroy the faith of the believers. Therefore, in this verse, Allah Almighty has warned that He will test His servants (with something from fear), that is, from fear of enemies and hunger, and from hunger, that is, from hunger and fear of enemies. They will be tested by something or the other, because if Allah makes them completely hungry and afraid, then they will perish, and trials and tests do not come for the purpose of killing, but for the purpose of purification. (وَنَقْصٍ مِّنَ الْمُوَالِ)" and from the lack of some wealth" includes all the lack and loss that causes the believers to suffer heavenly calamities, floods or drowning in the sea, the plundering of property by oppressors and the robbing of robbers. Occurs from And by the lack of lives, children, loved ones, relatives and friends, the servant himself tests them by causing illness to a believer or one of his loved ones. And by the lack of fruits. We will definitely test it by damaging grains, dates, vegetables and all fruit trees through hailstorms, cold, fire, celestial disasters and locusts. All these trials must come, because Allah Aalim wa Khabeer has informed about them and these trials happened in this way. When these tribulations occurred, people were divided into two categories. (1) Those who show impatience. (2) The patient ones.

The impatient person faced two miseries, the loss of the beloved object and the existence of that miseries. The second is to be deprived of something even greater, that is, not getting the reward while following what Allah has commanded patience, so loss, loss of fortune and loss of faith become his destiny. He loses patience, contentment and gratitude and gets in return resentment which indicates a severe loss.

But the person whom Allah Ta'ala blessed with patience at the time of these sufferings and hardships and he restrained himself from expressing anger towards Allah in word and deed. Then he hoped for a reward and reward from Allah Ta'ala and he also knows that the reward he will get from being patient is much more than the trouble he is facing, rather this trouble is his right. I am blessed, because this affliction has led to the attainment of that good and benefit which is better than this affliction. So he obeyed the command of Allah Ta'ala and was declared worthy of reward. Therefore, Allah Almighty said: "And give glad tidings to those who persevere." That is, give them the good news that Allah will reward them in full without any reckoning. So the people of patience are those who have been blessed with great tidings and a great reward.

Tafsir ahsanul bayan

2:156

To whom, when any trouble comes, they say that we are the property of Allah Almighty and we are going to return to Him.

Diseases and Conditions

Seasonal affective disorder (SAD)

Seasonal affective disorder (SAD) is a type of depression that's related to changes in the seasons - seasonal affective disorder (SAD) starts and ends at about the same time each year. If you're like most people with SAD, your symptoms begin in the fall and continue through the winter months, draining you of energy and making you feel moody. These symptoms often resolve during the spring and summer months. Less often, SAD causes depression in the spring or early summer and resolves during the fall or winter months.

Treatment for SAD can include light therapy (phototherapy), psychotherapy, and medications.

Don't brush off this annual feeling as just "winter blues" or seasonal blues that you have to deal with on your own. Take steps to keep your mood and motivation stable throughout the year.

Symptoms

In most cases, symptoms of seasonal affective disorder appear in late fall or early winter and fade in the sunny days of spring and summer. Less commonly, people with the opposite pattern have symptoms begin in spring or summer. In either case, symptoms may start out mild and become more severe as the season progresses.

Signs and symptoms of SAD may include:

Feeling sluggish, sad or hopeless most of the day, almost every day

Losing interest in activities you previously enjoyed

Having low energy and lethargy

Having trouble sleeping much

Craving for carbohydrates, overeating and gaining weight

Having difficulty concentrating

Feeling hopeless, worthless or guilty

Having thoughts of not wanting to live

Fall and winter SAD

Specific symptoms of winter SAD (sometimes called winter depression) may include:

Sleeping more

Changes in appetite, especially cravings for carbohydrate-rich foods

Weight gain

Fatigue or low energy

Spring and summer SAD

Specific symptoms of seasonal affective disorder, sometimes called summer depression, may include:

Insomnia

Inadequate appetite

Weight gain Events

Agitation or anxiety

Increased irritability

Seasonal changes and bipolar disorder

Sadness

"Sadness is an emotional pain associated with or characterized by feelings of loss, loss, despair, grief, helplessness, hopelessness, and sadness. A person experiencing sadness may become quiet or lethargic, and may isolate themselves from others. An example of severe sadness is depression, a mood that may be caused by major depressive disorder or persistent depressive disorder. Weeping may be a sign of sadness.

A detail of the 1672 sculpture Entombment of Christ, showing Mary Magdalene weeping

Sadness is one of the six basic emotions described by Paul Ekman, which also includes joy, anger, surprise, fear, and disgust. 271–4

Childhood

Sadness is a common experience in childhood. Sometimes, sadness can lead to depression. Some families may have a rule (conscious or unconscious) that sadness is "not allowed," but Robin Skinner has suggested that this can cause problems, arguing that keeping sadness "hidden" can make people shallow and frivolous. :33, 36Pediatrician T. Berry Brazelton suggests that acknowledging sadness can make it easier for families to address more serious emotional problems. :46, 48

Sadness is part of the child's normal process of separating from early symbiosis with the mother and becoming more independent. Each time the child separates a little more, he or she faces a small loss. If the mother cannot tolerate the minor distress involved, the child may never learn how to deal with sadness on his or her own. : 158–9 Brazelton argues that overly pleasing a child diminishes their ability to feel grief; : 52 and Selma Fraiberg suggests that it is important to respect the child's right to experience loss fully and deeply.

Margaret Mahler also saw the ability to feel sadness as an emotional achievement, as opposed to warding it off through restless hyperactivity, for example. D. W. Winnicott similarly saw in sad crying the psychological root of valuable musical experiences in later life.

Neuroanatomy

There has been a tremendous amount of research done on the neuroscience of sadness. According to the American Journal of Psychiatry, sadness has been found to be associated with "increased bilateral activity in the area surrounding the middle and posterior temporal cortex, lateral cerebellum, cerebellar vermis, midbrain, putamen, and caudate." José V. Pardo has an MD and PhD and leads a research program in cognitive neuroscience. Using positron emission tomography (PET), Pardo and his colleagues were able to induce sadness in seven normal men and women by asking them to think about sad things. They observed increased brain activity in the bilateral inferior and orbitofrontal cortex. In one study, a significant increase in activity was also observed in bilateral anterior temporal structures.

Coping mechanisms

(psychology)

A man expressing grief with his hands on his head

A carving of the family of Marija and Petar Skuljevic depicting grief over their death

People deal with sadness in different ways, and it is an important emotion because it helps motivate people to deal with their situation. Some coping methods include: seeking social support and/or spending time with a pet, making a list, or engaging in an activity to express grief. Some individuals, when feeling sad, may isolate themselves from social settings to allow time to recover from the emotion.

Although it is one of the mood states people most want to get rid of, sadness can sometimes persist due to chosen strategies such as ruminating, "drowning out one's sorrows," or isolating oneself forever. :69–70 As alternative ways to deal with sadness to the above, cognitive behavioral therapy instead suggests either challenging one's negative thoughts or scheduling some positive event to distract attention. :72

Being attentive to and patient with one's grief may also be a way for people to learn to cope through solitude; while emotional support to help people stay with their grief may be further helpful. :164 Such an approach is fueled by the underlying belief that loss (when felt wholeheartedly) can lead to a renewed sense of aliveness and re-engagement with the outside world.

Grief in Islam

Islam is a religion that respects human nature. Allah is aware of the emotions that people experience. For example, grief has a place in Islam and experiencing it is not discouraged.

There are many stories from Islam in which we see that there was grief. These stories confirm that it is okay to experience grief. The Prophet (ﷺ) experienced it, his companions and the scholars after him also experienced it.

Being sad is a natural emotion. It occurs in the event of accident, trauma, injustice and many other situations.

Furthermore, when Muslims experience a difficult situation, grief or anxiety their sins are forgiven.

The Prophet (ﷺ) said: "Never does a believer suffer from discomfort, difficulty, illness, grief and even anxiety, except that his sins are forgiven." [Sahih Muslim 2573]

Why me?"

In grief, that thought often comes to mind automatically, even if you try to stop it. It is a thought that tries to give a logical or reasonable explanation behind why you are in pain.

Allah tests any person with a calamity or difficulty that causes grief. Indeed, He wants the best for people. He expresses this in many verses of the Quran.

Allah wants ease for you and He does not want discomfort for you.

[2:185 Quran]

Allah wants to lighten your burden; and man is made weak.

[4:28 Quran]

You will not be tested beyond your ability

Sometimes it can be so difficult that you feel it is beyond your ability to deal with it. This happens when the test is very difficult. But Allah says that no one is tested beyond his ability.

Allah does not burden anyone beyond his ability.

[2:286 Quran]

Dealing with grief

There are different ways to deal with grief. So there are good and bad ways to deal with it. It is common for people to try to ignore grief, which can lead to depression.

Islam advises every Muslim to treat their grief. This is done by remembering Allah, among other things. But know that simply remembering Allah repeatedly is not the solution to grief.

Many people think that increasing faith, remembering Allah, or making dua is the solution to grief. This is not always the case, because grief is an emotional reaction, and therefore requires an emotional solution.

But how do you treat this emotional reaction with an emotional solution? What is that solution?

1. Find the cause

First, it is important to determine the cause of your grief. These can be different things.

Common causesLoss of loved ones

Parents who hurt you

Separation

Dismissal

Failure at school

The cause of your sadness determines its intensity. This will ensure that you can, for example, experience a deeper sadness.

Addressing the cause will give you a lot of clarity. This way you can understand it more precisely. Distress is an emotional response to a stressful event. Each person experiences an event differently. It has a greater impact on some people because sensitivity plays a role in it.

2. Give space to your sadness

The next step is to give yourself space to experience your sadness. So it is good that you express your sadness and give it the space it deserves.

To give space to your sadness, it is sometimes necessary to take a break from daily tasks. This way you give yourself time and space to experience your sadness.

Experiencing sadness is part of the release from the pain you are carrying. You reduce negative energy and stress in your body.

By experiencing your grief you open the door for the event to have less of an effect on you. You no longer feel as much pain as someone who ignores their grief.Extra: Talk to trustees

A natural action that we do when we are sad is to share it with people we trust. Sharing your story with someone else is very helpful. Expressing what is bothering you brings relief and clarification, as it reduces stress and pain.

The understanding and compassion that the trusted person gives you then ensures that you take the same approach to yourself. And that is the next step: compassion for yourself.

3. Compassion to restore

We often start judging ourselves after experiencing a negative event. This often happens automatically, but it has negative consequences.

When you judge yourself, you open the door to unnecessary guilt or criticism.

What compassion does is that it looks at your situation without judgment. It is a neutral perspective that removes unnecessary criticism or guilt.

The truth is that we are not always in control of our experience. For example, if you have lost a loved one or someone has done wrong to you, there is nothing you can do about it.When you had some control

Of course there are situations where you have the opportunity to change something. Think, for example, of failing school or getting fired from a job. We have some control over that, but if it happened unjustly, we can't. Then it's a matter of acknowledging that injustice has occurred.

We sometimes tend to criticize ourselves excessively. The result will be that we quickly sabotage the healing process.

The Purpose of Compassion

The purpose of offering compassion is not to degrade ourselves and be gentle with ourselves. We don't have full control, so we must drop that idea.

Sure, if you have wronged someone else, you have to put the blame on who it belongs to (yourself). Then you have to sort it out together with them.

Prayers for Suffering

Among other things, one can relieve suffering by praying. Many adiyya (plural of dua) are narrated. These were performed by the Prophet (ﷺ) and his companions.

The purpose of duas is a form of relief, remembrance of Allah and possible deliverance from suffering, difficulty and more.

Suffering cannot be relieved by merely making dua. You must also get to the core of the matter as you make dua.Ibn Abbas reported: The Prophet (ﷺ) said the following in a time of trouble: "There is no god except Allah, the All-Knowing, the Forbearing. There is no god except Allah, the Lord of the Exalted Throne. There is no god except Allah, the Lord of the heavens, the earth and the Exalted Throne." [Sahih al-Bukhari 7426, Sahih Muslim 2730]

The Prophet (ﷺ) said: "O Allah! I seek refuge in You from anxiety and grief, from incapacity and laziness, from cowardice and miserliness, from falling into heavy debt and from being oppressed by (other) people." [Sahih al-Bukhari 6369]

Stories of Grief in Islam

There are many Islamic stories that indicate that the Prophet (ﷺ) experienced grief. These stories provide validation for any Muslim experiencing grief.

These stories give you insight and understanding that grief is a natural response. The Prophet (ﷺ) went through many things in his life. For example, he lost his first wife Khadija and his beloved uncle Abu Talib in the same year.

The Year of Sorrow

This moment was a very difficult period in the life of the Prophet (ﷺ), also known as 'Am al-Huzn (the Year of Sorrow). He lost his first wife Khadija. She was the first person to believe in his prophethood.

Khadija accompanied the Prophet (ﷺ) during difficult times. She experienced this when the Prophet (ﷺ) first received revelation. Khadija was married to the Prophet (ﷺ) for 25 years. She died when the Prophet (ﷺ) was fifty years old.

After Khadija's death, Abu Talib: the beloved uncle of the Prophet (ﷺ). Abu Talib had a respected position among the Quraysh people.

His position gave him the power to protect his nephew Mohammed from his opponents. When Abu Talib died the Prophet (ﷺ) lost this protection and he never embraced Islam. Khadija and Abu Talib died in the same year. After Khadija's death, many difficulties arose. She provided solace and assistance to the Prophet in his becoming a prophet. With the death of Abu Talib, he lost support in his personal life and protection from the Quraish. Abu Talib died about three years before the Prophet migrated to Medina. During that time, the Quraish seized the opportunity to harm the Prophet. A man from the Quraish threw mud on the Prophet's (ﷺ) head. He returned to his home where he met his daughter. When she removed the mud from the Prophet's (ﷺ) head she wept, to which the Prophet (ﷺ) said: "Do not weep my daughter, Allah will protect your father. They (the Quraish) did not dare to harm me until Abu Talib died." [Sira of Ibn Hisham, "The Death of Khadija and Abu Talib"]

Death of Ibrahim

The Prophet (ﷺ) lost many of his children during his life. Of these children, son Ibrahim died.

We see in this story that the Prophet was also affected by trials. This proves his human nature and validates the experience of suffering in the life of a Muslim.

Anas bin Malik reported: We went with the Messenger of Allah (ﷺ) to Abu Saif the blacksmith, and he was the husband of the nursing wife of Ibrahim (the Prophet's son). The Messenger of Allah (ﷺ) took Ibrahim and kissed him and inhaled his fragrance. Later we went back to Abu Saif's house and at that moment Ibrahim breathed his last, and tears flowed from the eyes of the Messenger of Allah (ﷺ). Abdur Rahman bin Auf said: "O Messenger of Allah, you also cry!" The Messenger of Allah (ﷺ) said: "O Ibn Auf, this is mercy." Then Allah's Messenger (ﷺ) wept and said: "The eyes are shedding tears and the heart is grieved, and we will only say what our Lord pleases, O Ibrahim! Indeed we are grieved by your separation." [Sahih al-Bukhari 1303]Pause of Revelation

During the prophethood of Muhammad (ﷺ), the revelation was temporarily halted. This happened for some time which made the Prophet (ﷺ) worried and sad.

The disbelievers of the Quraish tried to put him down at that time. Thus they said that Allah stopped the revelation because He hated them.

The opponents tried every possible way to make the Prophet (ﷺ) sad. They said: "If this revelation had really come from Allah, it would have been continuous (without stopping), but Allah hates them and has left them."

The Prophet (ﷺ) was saddened by the words of the Quraish and their behavior with him. After this, the pause ended and Allah sent the revelation again.

Ibn Ishaq (the first Islamic historian) said: "Then the revelations ceased for some time, after which the Messenger of Allah (ﷺ) became worried and saddened. Then Jibril brought him Surat ad-Duha, in which his Lord, who had honored him so much, swore that he had not forgotten him, nor hated him." [Sira Ibn Hisham (1/225)]

Abu Athari

Abu Athari writes about the basic principles within Islam. He uses his critical and well-researched method to spread the knowledge of the first three Muslim generations.

My another books

Sr no.	Book
1	World's Major religions, doctrines and sects
2	An introduction to the Holy Qur'an and it's unsolved mysteries
3	How did humans and language originate ?
4	Islam an introduction and sect
5	Sermons of great people
6	Prayer
7	Allah an introduction
8	Is Al khizr still alive today?
9	Story of harut and marut
10	Grief
11	The mysterious story of Al kahf (Ar raqim)
12	Naming of God
13	Who was Sheeba?
14	Death concept of the Holy Quran

30	For Divorce! Who is responsible?
31	Hadith to denomination
32	Karma is the best?
33	According to dreams, religion and science
34	End day

<u>All these books are available in Hindi</u> language and other international languages and are also available in e-book for **<u>free on Google Play</u>** Store.

My personal introduction

My name is Abdul Waheed, my father's name is Late Haji Ubaidur Rahman and mother's name is Jaibunnisa. I have liked scientific ideology since childhood and have a calm nature and attachment to books. Due to which my curiosity interest has been continuously used in new discoveries and information. I got selected in polytechnic while doing BSc, but unfortunately it remained incomplete because father and brother died.

Two words of my father, which are very precious for my life,

<u>first - earn honestly, do not take support of lies,</u>

<u>secondly, respect food and eat as much as you want.</u> That's why the education remained incomplete due to the responsibility of the house, then later getting married. Still did not lose courage and

today the book is available in front of you in the form of my thoughts. If any information is left incomplete, please let us know.
Thank you .
Contact-
Abdul Waheed, Barabanki, Uttar Pradesh, India
https://www.facebook.com/profile.php?id=100091298026218